A Note on Endangered Species

We are losing our animals. More than 5,000 animal species are endangered or threatened worldwide. This means that they are in danger of disappearing forever.

To safeguard these animals, there are over 3,500 protected areas in the form of parks, wildlife refuges, and other reserves around the world. This book features ten of these endangered or threatened species.

We can all help save them by spreading the word about conservation.

The author wishes to thank Michael Sampson for his help in the preparation of this text.

Henry Holt and Company, LLC
Publishers since 1866
175 Fifth Avenue
New York, New York 10010
www.henryholtchildrensbooks.com

Library of Congress Cataloging-in-Publication Data
Martin, Bill
Panda bear, panda bear, what do you see? / by Bill Martin Jr; pictures by Eric Carle.
Summary: Illustrations and rhyming text present ten different endangered animals.
[1. Endangered species—Fiction. 2. Animals—Fiction. 3. Stories in rhyme.]
I. Carle, Eric, ill. II. Title.
PZ8.3.M3988 Pan 2003 [E]—dc21 2002010855
ISBN-13: 9780-8050-1758-8 / ISBN-10: 0-8050-1758-5
First Edition—2003
Printed in the United States of America on acid-free paper. ∞

10 9 8 7

Panda Bear, Panda Bear, What Do You See?

By Bill Martin Jr

Pictures by Eric Carle

Henry Holt and Company · New York

Panda Bear,
Panda Bear,
what do you see?

I see a bald eagle
soaring by me.

Bald Eagle,
Bald Eagle,
what do you see?

I see a water buffalo
charging by me.

Water Buffalo,
Water Buffalo,
what do you see?

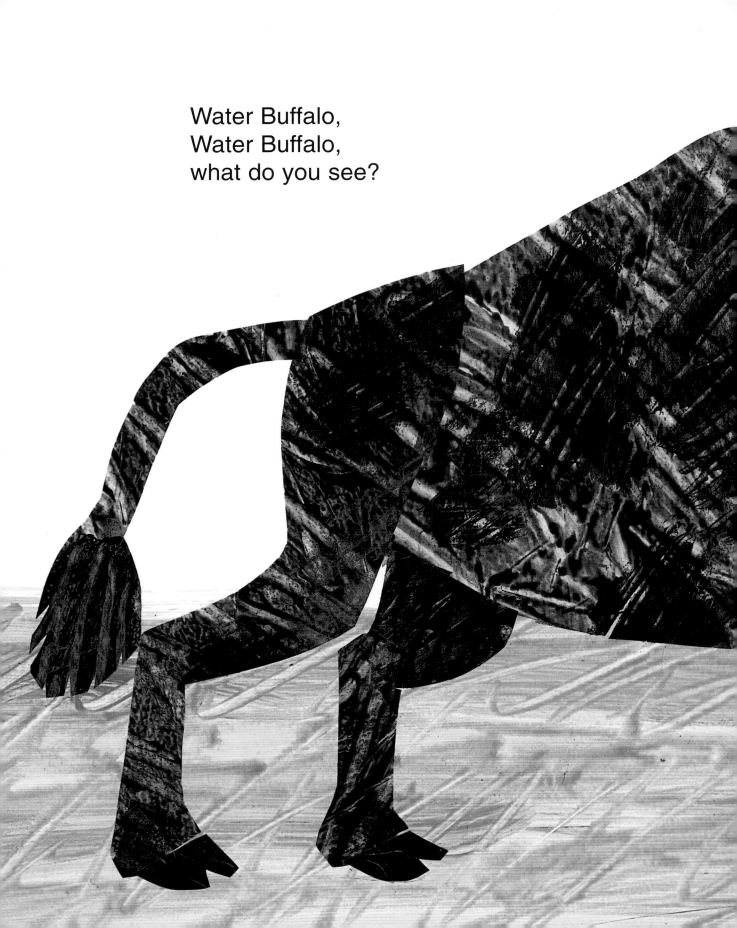

I see a spider monkey
swinging by me.

Spider Monkey,
Spider Monkey,
what do you see?

I see a green sea turtle
swimming by me.

Green Sea Turtle,
Green Sea Turtle,
what do you see?

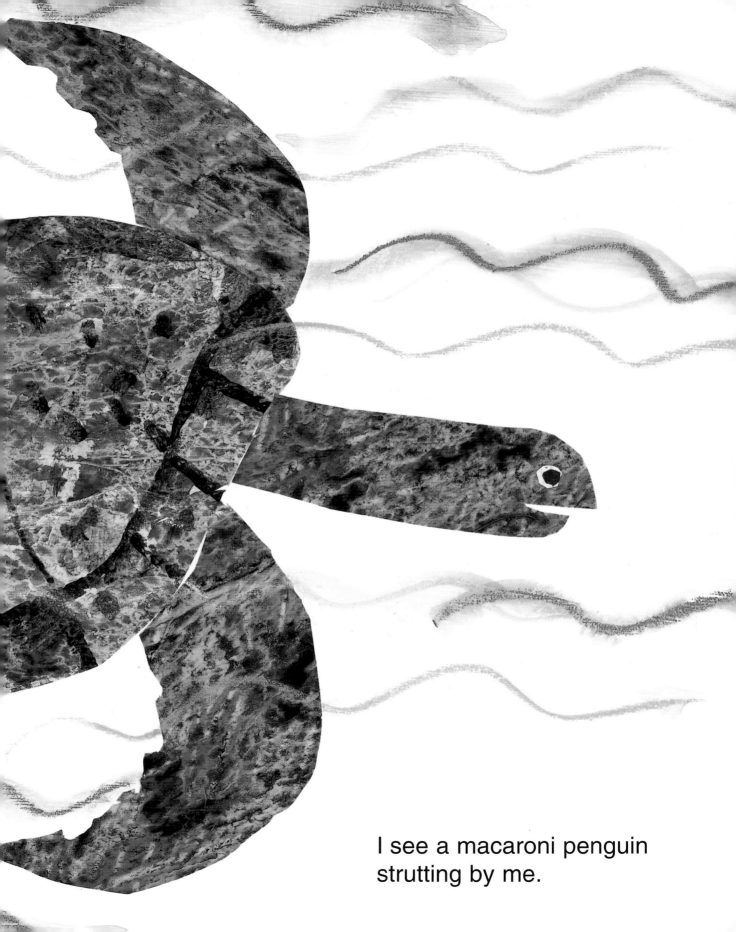

I see a macaroni penguin
strutting by me.

Macaroni Penguin,
Macaroni Penguin,
what do you see?

I see a sea lion
splashing by me.

Sea Lion,
Sea Lion,
what do you see?

I see a red wolf
sneaking by me.

Red Wolf,
Red Wolf,
what do you see?

I see a whooping crane
flying by me.

Whooping Crane,
Whooping Crane,
what do you see?

I see a black panther
strolling by me.

Black Panther,
Black Panther,
what do you see?

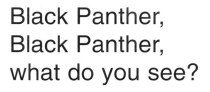

I see a dreaming child
watching over me.

Dreaming Child,
Dreaming Child,
what do you see?

I see . . .

a panda bear,

a spider monkey,

a green sea turtle,

a red wolf,

a whooping crane,

a bald eagle,

a water buffalo,

a macaroni penguin,

a sea lion,

and a black panther . . .

**all wild and free—
that's what I see!**